Based on the TV series *SpongeBob SquarePants*®
created by Stephen Hillenburg as seen on Nickelodeon®

An imprint of Simon & Schuster Children's Publishing Division
1230 Avenue of the Americas, New York, New York 10020

Manufactured in Mexico

First Edition

2 4 6 8 10 9 7 5 3 1

ISBN 0-689-85996-1

# Fish Happens!

by Tricia Boczkowski
illustrated by Caleb Meurer

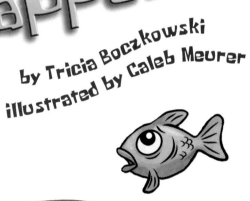

Simon Spotlight/Nickelodeon

New York · London · Toronto · Sydney · Singapore

I'm ready! (*Hit it, Gary.*)
It's time to bring it around town
because I'm getting my driver's license
today! And then I'm hitting the open
road. So long, Bikini Bottom! Hello,
Freedom! But First, the driving test . . .

# The bad news:

Mrs. Puff came down with a bad case of inflated nerves—not to mention sailor mouth!

# The good news:

She fit into the ambulance and got to ride around really fast with the siren on. Wheee!

# The bad news:

I had to resort to Plan B.

# The good news:

Plan B was a whole lot better than Plan BB!
I was ready to go on my very first road trip
with my very best friend, Patrick. It
doesn't get any better than that!

ding
ding
ding
ding

# The bad news:

We ran into a little bike trouble along the way. I could have sworn these tires used to touch the ground. . . .

# The good news:

Patrick remembered that he had a driver's license! And he even remembered how to drive.

# The bad news:

We got lost in a bad neighborhood and drove around in circles for hours.

# The good news:

We Found Atlantis!

# The bad news:

We couldn't find the boardwalk, the diving seahorse show, the Showboat casino, or the Miss Albacore Pageant.

Excuse me, sir, ...sir?

Hello?

# The good news:

We got back in the boat and kept driving.

# The bad news:

We got lost again and only had a map of Greater Bikini Bottom in the glove compartment.

# The good news:

We stumbled upon the Fish-out-of-Water Park.
Sandy would love it here!

# The bad news:

We couldn't get in.

# The good news:

We were having a great time just driving around! We listened to tunes, ate sandwiches, and made passing tugboats honk.

HONK!

# The bad news:

We wound up in a ghost town. I wonder if this is where the Flying Dutchman grew up. . . .

# The good news:

We found Bass Vegas! After chowing down at an all-you-can-eat buffet, Patrick and I took in the midnight show. (That Squiderace is amazing!) Then we played the slot machines for hours.

# The bad news:

We ran out of money ... and gas.

# The good news:

A nice man towed us home.
He even sang "Jailhouse Rock House"
and "Hound Dog Fish" for us!

# The bad news:

I'll miss the open road. I'll miss the adventures, the wind whistling through my pores, the endless blue ocean with all of its possibilities stretching out as far as the eye can see.

# The good news:

It's great to be home!
Aw, Gar-bear, I missed you too!